MAGIC MIRROR
with
MIDNIGHT FOREST

Through the magic mirror you will see; the Inca gold of the sunflower; hear the caressing song of the spider; and walk in the dreaming streets of Pompeii. You may even find yourself transformed . . .

MIDNIGHT FOREST
with
MAGIC MIRROR

What does a frog prince miss most? Why did the
teacher disappear? And most important of all, who
does wander the midnight forest?

The answers to these questions – and many
others – lie within . . .

by the same author

DRAGONSFIRE
and other poems
POPCORN PIE
(Mary Glasgow Publications)
HIGGLEDY-HUMBUG
(Mary Glasgow Publications)

edited by Judith Nicholls

WORDSPELLS
WHAT ON EARTH . . .?
Poems with a Conservation Theme
SING FREEDOM!

MIDNIGHT FOREST
with
MAGIC MIRROR

Judith Nicholls

ff

faber and faber
LONDON · BOSTON

First published in 1985
by Faber and Faber Limited
3 Queen Square London WC1N 3AU
This paperback reissue first published in 1993

Printed by Clays Ltd, St Ives plc

Judith Nicholls is hereby identified as the editor of this
work in accordance with Section 77 of the Copyright, Designs
and Patents Act 1988.

Cover illustration by
Shirley Felts

A CIP record for this book
is available from the British Library.
ISBN 0 571 16890 6

2 4 6 8 10 9 7 5 3 1

for John,
with love

CONTENTS

MIDNIGHT FOREST

Who wanders wild
in moon and puffball light
where night sleeps black
and spiders creep?
What is that sound
that stills the air?
Whose is the breath
that rustles oak and fir?
Beware,
the tree-gods stir.

SUPERSTITIONS

Wash your hands in the moonlight,
don't step on any crack;
cross your fingers,
cross your toes,
touch wood to keep your luck.

Always watch for black cats,
wear odd socks unawares;
choose sevens or threes,
'Bless you!' when you sneeze,
and never cross on stairs.

Remember these with all you've got;
                         if not .

WITCH'S CAT

is noiseless,
felt at dark
like silent breath;
stalker, not stalked,
a leaf or web
that brushes flesh,
the creak of empty stairs,
the cloud that darkens stars
and shrouds a moon.

Witch's cat
like fear, runs wild,
child of the shadows;
no child of light,
this silent cat of night.

CAT

My cat's tail
can dance or beckon
whilst he sleeps,
can wave or threaten,
fall or rise.

Warily
it lies awake,
all on its own;
he wakes,
it lies forgotten.
It lives a life alone,
quite separate –
or so it seems.

Could it be the place
where, secretly,
his life goes on?
A space to hide for ever
a million catty dreams?

DOG

Best friend?
Maybe!
Wiry hair-dropper,
four-legged yapper.
Sleep-disturber,
paws on the shoulders
and lick on the chin.
Unruly friend, sometimes.
I remember
Great Dane,
lolloping up stairs,
five-at-a-time
then sitting,
patient King of the Castle,
waiting for his slow
two-legged servant,
panting below.
Best friend!

WHO'S THERE?

Knock, knock!
Who's there?
cried the spider.
Stand and wait!
But she knew by the
gentle tweak of the web
it was her mate.

Knock, knock!
Who's there?
cried the spider.
Call your name!
But she knew by the
soft tap-tap on the silk
her spiderlings came.

Knock, knock!
Who's there?
cried the spider.
Who goes by?
But she knew by the
shaking of her net
it was the fly.

WOODLOUSE

Armoured dinosaur,
blundering through jungle grass by
dandelion-light.

Knight's headpiece, steel-hinged
orange-segment, ball-bearing,
armadillo-drop.

Pale peppercorn, pearled
eyeball; sentence without end,
my rolling full-stop.

TIGER

Tiger, eyes dark with
half-remembered forest night,
stalks an empty cage.

WOLF

still on his lone rock
stares at the uncaged stars and
cries into the night.

DEAR NOAH . . .

Moth

One corner of the ark –
a mulberry leaf to fly on,
lay on, eat from, lie on;
and please, a firefly, just one,
to dance around at dark.

Sloth

I like this floating bed –
the warm smell of animal,
a log to swing on
as the clouds drift by.
Supper is brought
and all day long
the seagull-cry
and sigh of lapping waves,
my lullaby.

Worm

Give me a hole to slither in,
rain for wallowing, soil for swallowing
and not too many fishermen with hooks.

Please, Noah.

TORTOISE AND HARE POEM

(or: Slow, slow, quick, quick, slow . . .)

Slowly the tortoise raised her head,
stared slowly at the hare;
slowly stepped towards the line
and waited there.

Calmly she heard the starting gun,
crawled calmly down the track;
calmly watched the hare race on
with arching back.

Quickly the hare ran out of sight,
chased quickly through the wood;
quickly fled through fern and moss,
through leaf and mud.

Swiftly he leapt past hedge and field,
sped swiftly for his prize;
briefly stopped to take a rest –
and closed his eyes.

Slowly the tortoise reached the wood,
slowly she ambled on.
The hare raced proudly through his dreams;
the tortoise won.

READY, STEADY? NO!

My Dad's
a keep-fit fiend.
You know,

press-ups and sit-ups,
jogging and squash;
toe-touch and leg-stretch,
lunch on the dash.
No time for an old-fashioned
ploughman's and beer,
'The pool's open now,
we can sprint it from here!'

Even on Sundays
he's up with the lark:
tennis in summer,
weights after dark.
Arms bend and neck twist,
runs on the spot,
scissor-jumps, rugby –
he does the lot.

As for me,
I *hate* sport,
prefer bed until three;
a mere game of draughts
is exhausting to me.
He'll always hike;
well, I'll join the queue
and travel by train,
as we were meant to!

SISTER

Tell me a story!
Lend me that book!
Please, let me come in your den?
I won't mess it up,
so *please* say I can.
When? When? When?

Lend me that engine,
that truck – and your glue.
I'll give half of my old bubblegum.
You know what Dad said
about learning to share.
Give it *now* –
or I'm telling Mum!

Oh, *please* lend your bike –
I'll be careful this time.
I'll keep out of the mud
and the snow.
I could borrow your hat –
the one you've just got . . .

                    said my sister.

And I said

                    NO!

ADVICE

Do put a coat on,
and fasten that shoe.
I'd take a sweater,
      if I were you . . .

It's chilly at nights now,
you're bound to catch 'flu;
I'd button up warmly,
      if I were you . . .

Please yourself if you must
but I know what *I'd* do;
I'd stay at home now,
      if I were you . . .

The nights have drawn in,
you never know who
might be lurking out there
      just waiting for you . . .

I don't know what the youth
of today's coming to!
They do what they like
      and like what they do!

Now when *I* was young,
it caused hullaballoo
if I stayed out past nine –
      and I never dared to.

If I were young now,
I know what *I'd* do . . .

*I'd enjoy every minute
if I were you!*

MUM AND DAD...

Weather wet,
food bad;
send cash
please Dad.

Sick on coach
(only twice)
Bill shares tent
(got headlice).

Field's a bog,
full of flies;
local bull
quite a size.

Wellies pinched,
sweaters gone;
walked to town
on my own.

Sir still drunk,
fell in bin –
by the way,
I like gin!

Enjoy your rest,
have a ball,
relaxez-vous
one and all.

Better stop,
doing the town.

See you soon,
love from John.

p.s. *Forget cash,*
raid's on!
Must dash –
loving son.

xxxxxxx

I'M A VEGGIE

The day my Mum
went vegetarian
we ate

cabbage and carrot
and juicy nut stew,
peanut and chestnut,
pistachio, cashew;
yoghurt with honey,
sesame thins,
peas, beans and pumpkin
(out went the tins!)
Dates, grapes, bananas,
lentils, cheese pie,
potatoes, tomatoes . . .
We thought we would die
without our chip fix,
our sausage and mash,
greasy bacon, beefburgers,
thick cornbeef hash . . .

Funny thing was,
she went off for a week.
'Quick, the butcher!' cried Dad,
keen to give us a treat.
We stuffed ourselves silly
on turkey and ham,
on roast beef and gravy
and pink fatty Spam;
bacon with breakfast,
lamb's leg for lunch,
pork scratchings for snacks

when we needed a munch.
After six days of that . . .

We just couldn't wait
for a huge pile of beetroot
and prunes on our plate!
We forgot about beef
and all made solemn pledges
from that day to this
to be long-crunching veggies!

RUSH HOUR

Nine o'clock,
the bell has gone!
Walk in quietly;
Tim, lead on . . . . . .

And the whole of Class Four
make a dash for the door:
scuttle and scurry,
hurtle and flurry,
jotter and tostle,
stragger and hastle;
muscle and bolting,
bolliding and sholting,
beap, sweep and jumble,
shunt, shove and trundle,
swallop and chase . . .
You'd never have guessed
from the way that they race

they all HATE SCHOOL!

NICE WORK

Never use the word NICE,
            our teacher said.
It doesn't mean a thing!
Try . . .
beautiful, shining, delicious,
shimmering, hopeful, auspicious,
attractive, unusual, nutritious –
the choice is as long as a string!
But please, *never* use the word NICE,
it just doesn't mean a thing!

(*She's nice, our teacher.*)

BULLY

Slowly he straightened his back,
ran chewed stumps through his hair;

slowly he straightened leathered knees
and got up from his chair.

Slowly he fixed me with his eye
(I dared not leave his glare);

slowly he reached to his pocket,
put something there.

Slowly he stepped towards me,
his mouth curled in a grin;

slowly, slowly, he came closer...
Quickly...I RAN!

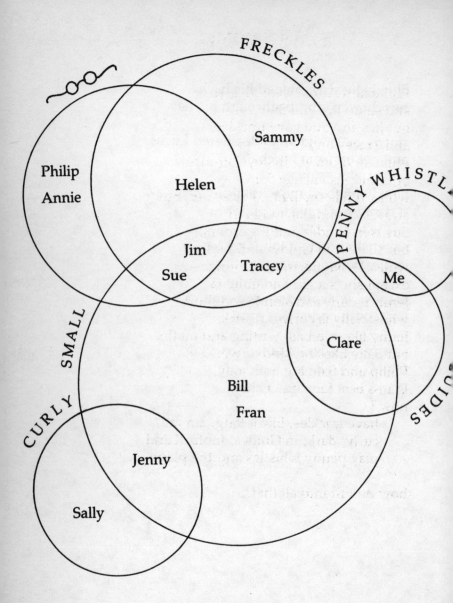

CLASSIFYING

Philip and Annie wear glasses
and so do Jim and Sue,
but Jim and Sue have freckles,
and Tracey and Sammy too.
Philip and Jim are in boys' group
but Philip is tall like Sam
whilst Jim is small like Tracey and Sue
and Clare and Bill and Fran.
Sue is in Guides and Recorders,
but Clare is in Guides and football
whilst Helen fits in most things –
except she's a girl and quite tall.
Jenny is curly and blonde and short
whilst Sally is curly but dark;
Jenny likes netball, writing and maths
but Sally likes no kind of work.
Philip and Sam are both jolly,
Fran's best for a quiet chat;
now I
    have freckles, like joking, am tall,
    curly, dark, in Guides, football and
    play penny whistles and the piano . . .

how do *I* fit into all that?

THE EXPERIMENT

I want you to think,
said sir,
about *nothing*,
sir said.
Empty your head;
sit dead still,
don't move a toe
until I say so.
Ready? – *Go!*

It's easy not to blink –
you'd think.
First I blinked.
Then I saw Gary Flynn
pinching his lips
to keep the giggle in.
My big toe wiggled,
Kevin Nuttall wriggled,
Mary Bollom sneezed,
the clown!
I could see sir
trying hard to frown
without moving his face.
I squeezed my toes,
Kevin Nuttall froze
and Mary Bollom went red.
I tried hard to sit still
and c-o-n-c-e-n-t-r-a-t-e
as *nothing*
rushed through my head.

PARTNERS

Find a partner,
says sir, and sit
with him or her.
A whisper here,
a shuffle there,
a rush of feet.
One pair,
another pair,
till twenty-four
sit safely on the floor
and all are gone
but one
who stands,
like stone,
and waits;
tall,
still,

alone.

THE DARE

Go on, I dare you,
come on down!

Was it *me* they called?
Pretend you haven't heard,
a voice commanded in my mind.
Walk past, walk fast
and don't look down,
don't look behind.

Come on, it's easy!

The banks were steep,
the water low
and flanked with oozing brown.
Easy? Walk fast
but don't look down.
Walk straight, walk on,
even risk their jeers
and run . . .

Never go near those dykes,
my mother said.
No need to tell me.
I'd seen stones sucked in
and covered without trace,
gulls slide to bobbing safety,
grasses drown as water rose.
No need to tell me
to avoid the place.

She ca-a-a-n't, she ca-a-a-n't!

Cowardy, cowardy custard!

There's no such word as 'can't',
my father said.
I slowed my pace.
The voices stopped,
waited as I wavered, grasping breath.
My mother's wrath? My father's scorn?
A watery death?

I hesitated then turned back,
forced myself to see the mud below.
After all, it was a dare . . .
There was no choice;
I had to go.

VILLAGE SCHOOL

A stile, a field,
some dozen cows
and then the church.
A muddy dyke,
some silver roach
and just below the bridge
a sharp-toothed pike
which lurks alone
for small unwary stragglers,
whispering doom.

The school, one room.
Beneath high-windowed stone
fixed smiling in her chair
the kindly Mrs Mullins,
large in blue and black
with neatly-curlered hair.
From nine to twelve
and later on till three
she calls our fate
and welcomes all
on ample knee.
A scratch of slate,
a shuffle here or there,
a child in late;
chalk-dusted autumn
clouds the air.

At last a break. Wait
unwillingly for bottled milk,
cool in its rattling crate,
then under teacher's watchful eye

lace-up for play.
Scarves, coats and hopscotch
when the weather's dry
and crying at the gate for home
under a grey Lincolnshire sky.

A LINCOLNSHIRE
NURSERY RHYME

Boston, Wainfleet,
Haxey, Hogsthorpe, Well;
Weston, Westborough,
Thorpe, Brigg, Hale.

Old Leake and Mumby,
Osbournby, Fleet,
Old Bolingbroke, Leverton,
Bourne, Lea, Wroot.

POACHED EGG

Huttoft, Dunsby, Sapperton, Well,
Haxey, Dowsby, Hacconby, Haugh;
Addlethorpe, Harrington, Asgarby, Waith,
Cumberworth, Holdingham, Gautby, Lea, Knaith.

BIKING

Fingers grip,
toes curl;
head down,
wheels whirl.

Hair streams,
fields race;
ears sting,
winds chase.

Breathe deep,
troubles gone;
just feel
windsong.

SONG OF THE FROG PRINCE

It's the royal bed I miss.
Oh, I can do without
the state occasions,
the bowing and the handshakes,
the gold crown, weighting my head.
All those unwanted presents
to be grateful for,
and far too many strawberries,
out-of-season.
But the royal bed . . .
pillows, soft with silk,
deep, feathered mattresses
with satin sheets,
quilts billowing with eider.

A kiss, dear lady, please.
Just one small kiss.

DAVID AND GOLIATH

David was a shepherd boy,
Jesse's youngest son;
watched his sheep,
played his harp,
practised with his sling.
He learned to cast a pebble
through the mountain air;
a loin cloth was his armour.
From lion, jackal, bear
he rescued Jesse's sheep alone.
He knew no fear.

His king was Saul,
a brave one
who kept the Philistines at bay;
bold in battle any day,
he later came to disobey
and was undone.

Saul, Saul,
your mood is black;
call for the boy
with the magic harp.

The shepherd boy lay dreaming
in the summer grass
when they called him to the palace
to help Saul's dark dreams pass.
His music calmed the troubled king
who smiled to hear his song;
but meantime
on the mountainside
the Philistines marched on.

Saul, Saul,
your champion please
to fight our giant, fast!

Across the valley
stood Goliath,
bristling, vast.

Goliath rang,
an iron man:
helmet, brass,
coat of mail,
breastplate, legplates,
spear and shield.
Ten feet tall,
spearshaft wide
as any arm
on that mountainside.

I'll fight this man,
said David.
King Saul was full of doubt
but they set him up in plates of brass,
quite sure that he had breathed his last
and sent him out.

The shepherd boy
took off his mail,
took off his shield and sword.
I fought a lion with God's help,
I'm safe with just His word.
Goliath is no jackal
though he hides in a coat of mail,
and might's not right

in every fight;
I shall not fail.

Goliath looked. He stared.
He laughed. He roared.
His legplates shook,
his army cheered.

Goliath jeered

I'll give your flesh
to the fowls of the air,
your heart
to the beasts of the field;
your liver will fill
some roaming bear
when I've wiped you
off my shield!
Where is your sword,
vile midget?
Are you really
the best they could find?
Step forward,
let's finish this quickly!
I'll grind your bones
like summer wheat
and scatter your chaff
to the wind!

But David stood.

He heard the Philistines' laughter,
he heard Goliath's jeer;
the giant's metal music rang
discordant in his ear.

He picked five stones
from a nearby stream;
swung one, flung one, stood . . .
it arched like Noah's rainbow
then caught the giant's head.
He fell like a dove to the mountainside.
His army scattered like chaff as they cried
Goliath's dead!

David was a shepherd boy,
Jesse's youngest son;
slew Goliath,
saved his country –
with a stone.

JONAH'S LAMENT

Dark, only dark,
with only hands for eyes;
saved – for a life of touch!
Is *this* my end,
fumbling at some bony stalactite
inside this dank, rank cave?
What scaffold props my roof,
curves out damp walls,
all velvet-hung?
Moist flesh,
indenting to my touch,
closes like giant clam,
a curling tongue.
Some swallowed, mucus-tacky fish
noses its scaly length about my neck,
lost in the slap of falling sea.
Salt rinses mouth and lips
and all around the stench
of half-digested fish
breathes over me.

PERSEPHONE

Lay down your poppies
   red with sun,
   beneath the judas-tree;
   beware the black-horsed lord of night,
   Persephone.

Bury your violets
   with the shades,
   drink deep the black, black sea;
   ferry your corn to Dis's cave,
   Persephone.

Fasten your veil with
   lilies pale,
   dull nightshade dim your eyes;
   under sad lilac make your grave,
   till winter dies.

STORYTIME

Once upon a time, children,
there lived a fearsome dragon . . .

Please, miss,
Jamie's made a dragon.
Out in the sandpit.

Lovely, Andrew.
Now this dragon
had enormous red eyes
and a swirling, whirling tail . . .

Jamie's dragon's got
yellow eyes, miss.

Lovely, Andrew.
Now this dragon was
as wide as a horse
as green as the grass
as tall as a house . . .

Jamie's would JUST fit
in our classroom, miss!

But he was a very friendly dragon . . .

Jamie's dragon ISN'T, miss.
He eats people, miss.
Especially TEACHERS,
Jamie said.

Very nice, Andrew!

Now one day, children,
this enormous dragon
rolled his red eye,
whirled his swirly green tail
and set off to find . . .

His dinner, miss!
Because he was hungry, miss!

Thank you, Andrew.
He rolled his red eye,
whirled his green tail,
and opened his wide, wide mouth
until

Please, miss,
I did try to tell you, mi

LEARNING TO SWIM

Today I am
dolphin-over-the-waves,
roach and stickleback,
silver mermaid,
turning tide,
ribbon-weed
or sprat.

Water drifts through my mind;
I twist, I glide,
leave fear behind in sand,
wander a land
of turtle, minnow, seal
where whale is king.

Today – I swim!

SEA DREAM

I wander the deep-sea forests
where the snake-fish slither;
where the dark dunes drift
like rolling mist
and the white whales murmur.

I wake to coral blossom
and sleep in a star-clad cave;
my bed is a glade
of ribboned jade,
my sky a wave.

I dance by the spiny urchin
and ride the giant clam;
I feel as I sail
the dolphin's tail
the sad whale song.

MARY CELESTE

Only the wind sings
in the riggings,
the hull creaks a lullaby;
a sail lifts gently
like a message
pinned to a vacant sky.
The wheel turns
over bare decks,
shirts flap on a line;
only the song of the lapping waves
beats steady time . . .

First mate,
off-duty from
the long dawn watch, begins
a letter to his wife, daydreams
of home.

The Captain's wife is late;
the child did not sleep
and breakfast has passed . . .
She, too, is missing home;
sits down at last to eat,
but can't quite force
the porridge down.
She swallows hard,
slices the top from her egg.

The second mate
is happy.
A four-hour sleep,
full stomach
and a quiet sea

are all he craves.
He has all three.

Shirts washed and hung, beds
made below, decks done, the boy
stitches a torn sail.

The Captain
has a good ear for a tune;
played his child to sleep
on the ship's organ.
Now, music left,
he checks his compass,
lightly tips the wheel,
hopes for a westerly.
Clear sky, a friendly sea,
fair winds for Italy.

The child now sleeps, at last,
head firmly pressed into her pillow
in a deep sea-dream.

Then why are the gulls wheeling
like vultures in the sky?
Why was the child snatched
from her·sleep? What drew
the Captain's cry?

Only the wind replies
in the rigging,
and the hull creaks and sighs;
a sail spells out its message
over silent skies.
The wheel still turns
over bare decks,

shirts blow on the line;
the siren-song of lapping waves
still echoes over time.

A POEM FOR THE RAINFOREST

Song of the Xingu Indian

They have stolen my land;
the birds have flown,
my people gone.
My rainbow rises over sand,
my river falls on stone.

Amazonian Timbers, Inc.

This can go next –
here, let me draw the line.
That's roughly right,
give or take
a few square miles or so.
I'll list the ones we need.
No, burn the rest.
Only take the best,
we're not in this
for charity.
Replant? No –
you're new to this, I see!
There's plenty more
where that comes from,
no problem! Finish here –
and then move on.

Dusk

Butterfly, blinded
by smoke, drifts like torn paper
to the flames below.

Shadows

Spider,
last of her kind,
scuttles underground, safe;
prepares her nest for young ones. But
none come.

The Coming of Night

Sun sinks
behind the high canopy;
the iron men are silenced.

The moon rises,
the firefly wakes.
Death pauses for a night.

Song of the Forest

*Our land has gone,
our people flown.
Sun scorches our earth,
our river weeps.*

SEASON SONG

Spring stirs slowly, shuffles, hops;
Summer dances close behind.
Autumn is a jostling crowd
but Winter creeps into your mind.

DANDELION IN WINTER

Where now, my
sleepyhead, old lion's teeth,
bold wet-the-bed?
Sly stowaway, why hide away
your golden wine
till leafy May?
No mirrored stars
for chill December fields?
Where did it go,
your time-tell summer snow
now winter's come?
Your molten suns
lie buried, cold
and yet . . .
you whisper
from your silent world,
volcano-rumbles
caging summer power.
A thousand traitors
lurk in earth's damp cellar,
wait till March gives in;
then every spring . . .
You win, you win, you win!
My phantom sower,
sparkler-shower,
heart-of-iron,
dandelion!

WINTER

Winter crept
through the whispering wood,
hushing fir and oak;
crushed each leaf and froze each web –
but never a word he spoke.

Winter prowled
by the shivering sea,
lifting sand and stone;
nipped each limpet silently –
and then moved on.

Winter raced
down the frozen stream,
catching at his breath;
on his lips were icicles,
at his back was death.

ROOM AT THE INN

Draughty, husband, that stable.
She looked . . . warm, though.
Almost at home.
And you know, husband, I swear
it's not one mite as dark in there
as you'd have thought.
And that child – so still, so quiet.
Perhaps they'll need more straw?
It won't get any warmer, early hours.
Maybe we should bring them in?
Husband, you're not listening!

There is our bed . . .
but then with breakfast early
and so many travellers . . .
Well, *they* won't go tomorrow, surely?
Husband, did you see . . .?
Husband!
Oh well, old man, dream on!
Some day we've had,
and then those two arriving,
with every nook and cranny gone!

Funny how those moths
circled the old lantern,
husband. Almost like . . .
almost as if those three . . .
but no, it couldn't be!
And the light,
you should have seen the light!
Oh, it flickered, but
so bright, so bright,

and night so still.
Draughty it is, that stable,
husband.

DECEMBER

W   ater

I   ces

N   aked

T   rees;

E   arth

R   ests.

MAGIC MIRROR
with
MIDNIGHT FOREST

Judith Nicholls

ff

faber and faber

LONDON · BOSTON

First published in 1987
by Faber and Faber Limited
3 Queen Square London WC1N 3AU
This paperback reissue first published in 1993

Printed by Clays Ltd, St Ives plc

Judith Nicholls is hereby identified as the editor of this
work in accordance with Section 77 of the Copyright, Designs
and Patents Act 1988.

Cover illustration by
Shirley Felts

A CIP record for this book
is available from the British Library.
ISBN 0 571 16890 6

2 4 6 8 10 9 7 5 3 1

For Dominique,
Guy and Tracey
with love

Contents

ALL ABOARD!

Hurry! cried Noah,
and into the ark
rushed

the osprey and the otter
the ostrich and the ox,
the jackal, kangaroo and kite
the scorpion and the fox.
The cacomistle, fresh from sleep
inside his hollow tree,
the cockroach and the cockatoo
the whistling chickadee.
The leopard and the tiger
the squat-nosed liverfluke,
the slow-worm and the glow-worm
and the shy young snake-eyed sheik.
Hinny, hippo, hobby,
hyena, hare and horse,
they all rushed over Noah's plank
before the storm broke loose.

Come in, come in! cried Noah,
Firefly, light these cloudy skies!
In crept grass-snake and glass-snake,
begging birds and mice.

Welcome mealybug and barnacle
and you too, leaf-nosed bat!
Do watch the step – our table's set,
the meal is steaming hot.
I only hope – these skies are black –
our simple ark won't fail!
The swan flew in disdainfully
with Chinese-painted quail.

Oh firefly, light our cloudy skies!
Do come in, mole and rat.
If God is willing, here's your home
beside Mount Ararat.

NIGHT

There's a dark, dark wood
inside my head
where the night owl cries;
where clambering roots
catch at my feet
where fox and bat
and badger meet
and night has eyes.

There's a dark, dark wood
inside my head
of oak and ash and pine;
where the clammy grasp
of a beaded web
can raise the hairs
on a wanderer's head
as he stares alone
from his mossy bed
and feels
the chill of his spine.

There's a dark, dark wood
inside my head
where the spider weaves;
where the rook rests
and the pale owl nests,
where moonlit bracken
spikes the air
and the moss is covered,
layer upon layer,
by a thousand fallen leaves.

FISHING SONG

Ragworm, lugworm, mackerel, maggot,
Grey pike lurking, still as steel.
Cast my rod in the deep dark stream
With a nugget of bread for a silver bream.

                            Caught an eel.

Ragworm, lugworm, mackerel, maggot,
Number Ten hook and I'm waiting still.
A carp would be good or a spiny perch,
A golden rudd or a red-finned roach?

                               It's an eel.

Ragworm, lugworm, mackerel, maggot,
Something's biting, wind up the reel!
Is it a pike or a roach or a rudd?
A hunting gudgeon from the river bed?

                            Just – an eel.

BALLAD OF THE SAD ASTRONAUT

Why are you weeping, child of the future,
For what are you grieving, son of the earth?
Acorns of autumn and white woods of winter,
Song-thrush of spring in the land of my birth.

You have a new life, child of the future,
Drifting through stars to a land of your own.
With Sirius to guide you, Orion beside you
Wandering the heavens you are free from earth's
                                                    harm.

I have a new life, the speckled skies' beauty,
Left far behind me the dark cries of earth;
Oh, but I long for the soft rains of April,
Ice-ferned Decembers and suns of the south.

What was I dreaming, to drift with Orion,
To leave for cold Neptune my home and my hearth?
Stars in their millions stretch endless, remind me
Far far behind lies my blue-marbled earth.

Here on the hillside the dawn is just rising,
Buttercups dew-fill, all silken and gold.
Well may you weep, sad child of the future,
Well may you yearn for your beautiful world.

MOONSCAPE

No air, no mist, no man, no beast.
No water flows from her Sea of Showers,
no trees, no flowers fringe her Lake of Dreams.
No grass grows or clouds shroud her high hills
or deep deserts. No whale blows in her dry
                            Ocean of Storms.

MIDAS

'The touch of gold!'
King Midas boldly craved.
Eyes glittered as he ran
from Bacchus' mountain cave
to find a golden land
where purple grape and twig of oak,
sleek lizard, stone and waving corn
like golden apples of the sun
all gilded to his stroke.

'A golden future!'
Midas cried
upon his golden throne.
And scarlet rose with olive branch,
plump aubergine and fragrant grass
passed through his grasping Judas kiss
to dazzle in the sun.

'Bring on the feast!'
King Midas laughed,
reached out for wine and bread;
raised his glass to take a sip
but when the red wine touched his lip
King Midas understood.

Oh gold was my corn and green my vine
and red was my wine of old;
never again shall I pine for wealth
or crave a richer world.

Lord Bacchus took pity, freed the king
from the gift he had longed to hold;
yet Autumn comes still with its Midas touch,
turns all to dying gold.

WORDHUNTER

My brother chases frogs –
well, eggs to be precise,
that jelly-baby spawn
which lurks near murky weed
after the winter's ice.
Takes them from the very doors
of hairy water-boatmen's jaws.
But me,
I'm a wordhunter.

Now my uncle,
he hunts butterflies.
Searches nettles, heaps of dung
for Purple Emperors, cabbage white,
Swallowtails with painted wing –
I'm sure you know the kind of thing.
Not me,
I'm a wordhunter.

See my sister Sue.
She chases – daydreams.
Laugh or tease, she just replies
'What do I care?'
Closes eyes and quickly flies
back to her castles in the air.
Not me,
I'd rather be

A WORDHUNTER.

14

WORDHUNTER'S COLLECTION

There's wiggle and giggle
goggles and swatch,
straggle and gaggle
and toggle and itch.

Glimmering, shimmering,
glistening, twinkle,
poppycock, puddle
and muddle and pimple.

Peapod and flip-flop,
rickety, dodo,
murmuring, lingering,
galaxy, yo-yo.

Extra-terrestrial's
one that I love,
Betelgeuse, Pluto –
Heavens above!

Who would not fall
for a bird called a chickadee?
A widgeon or warthog
or just the old chimpanzee?

Many's the word
that I capture each day,
whispering each
till I know it will stay.

Safely they sit
in my wordhunter's store –
and when I feel hungry
I wordhunt for more.

JONAH

Jonah was a later one
among God's prophets,
not one to be sat upon,
didn't do as asked;
you could even say, alas,
he was rather like a
naughty little boy!
Off you go to Nineveh,
said God one day, Your task
to tell them that
I know about their
wickedness. In forty days
I shall destroy.

So did our Jonah move?
No.
He thought along these lines:
God is loving, he'll forgive,
give a second chance, let live.
Will He really kill?
I don't believe He will!
They'll all think I've gone mad,
I *won't* do as He says,
it really is too bad!

So off he went,
but not to Nineveh;
caught a boat for Spain in
Jaffa's port. Can you blame him?

Out at sea,
the storm began.
Full of fear and shaking to a man,
the sailors, terrified, began to pray.
Jonah slept.
Pray, the captain cried.
What can I say, cried Jonah in dismay.
God sent this storm because I ran away.
Throw me overboard, said Jonah,
then the loving Lord, said Jonah,
will sooth the savage seas.
And all the sailors wept.

At last they threw him over in alarm,
watched in wonder as the angry seas grew calm.
Every sailor and his captain out of harm
now gave a prayer of thanks to this new God.
But what of Jonah?

The grey waves rose over him,
the wild waves closed over him,
he called to God for help.
Yes, his Lord had followed him,
sent a fish which swallowed him!
Safe inside the whale he wallowed in
despair.

Alone, afraid and sad,
for three dark days he stayed
inside the murky cavern of the whale.
Jonah thought;
wished he never had
ignored his only God,
felt it wrong he'd been
so mad and said,
well – sorry, Lord.
Would he live to tell his sorry tale?

At last the time was come.
With a wriggle and a shlurp
and a tidal wave of burp
the whale now cast out
Jonah on a beach.
With danger out of reach
he thanked the Lord for sun.

Straight away
he went to Nineveh,
took the message to the people,
and the people, they believed;
changed their ways so utterly
that God did not destroy them
and – can you guess? – Yes!
Jonah felt aggrieved.

Sat down outside the city,
moaned he'd known
what God would do; gave a sigh
half full of anger, half self-pity,
asked God now to leave him there to die.

God said no.
Sent a plant to grow
and shade him from the desert sun,
made him feel much better yet again.
But then
                next day
                            the plant
                                    began
                                        to die.

I liked that plant,
said Jonah, sad; I'm
sorry that it's gone.
I may seem just a moaner, but
I just don't understand.
You are sorry for a plant,
I was sorry for a nation
that I'd given life, said God.
I saw that in their fashion
they had learnt.

And Jonah,
head in hand
on that gold and burning sand
began to think,
began to feel,
began to see.

At last, he said, I think I understand.

ANDROMEDA

On a mole-black night when the stars are bright
And the cloud-veiled moon is high,
If you search near the wings of Pegasus
You can see her in the sky.

Chained fast to a rock, she waits her fate
As the great sea-monster's prey;
As she hides in fear she can hear the hiss
Of Cetus on his way.

But wait, it's the swish of Pegasus' wings
With Perseus riding high!
On a mole-black night with the stars in flight
You can see them ride away.

UNCLE WILLIAM

I stayed with you once
in your tiny church-lane cottage
with the outside pump, the velvet cloth
and sing-songs cramped around the piano.

With black-fringed stumps of fingers,
braces, ample paunch,
you could have been
miner, dustman, sweep –
but no, village blacksmith
fitted best that village scene.

I remember strong green soap,
tin bowls of icy water for the morning wash;
my aunt's night-calling for the cat
across still hedgerows and the cobbled lane,
a shared bed with spoiling cousins,
Billy Bunter by oil lamp at forbidden hours
and orange moths against the darkened pane.

Uncle William. Dead now;
the blacksmith and the cottage gone.
No cobbled lane but just a road now,
a road my aunt must tread alone.

DREAM OF THE FAIR FOREST

by
Judith Nicholls

Where can I hide in you,
forest, fair forest?
Where can I hide in you,
forest so green?

Hide in my pine trees,
my beeches, my aspen.
Hide in my maples,
where none can be seen.

How shall I live in you,
forest, fair forest?
How shall I live in you,
forest so gay?

Live on my berries,
my cobnuts, my rosehips.
Live on my blackberries,
they'll last many-a-day.

Who shall I live with,
oh forest, fair forest?
Who shall I live with,
my forest so wild?

Live with my squirrels,
my nuthatch, my night owls.
Live with my badgers
and live as my child.

What shall I lie on,
green forest, my forest?
What shall I lie on
when night starts to fall?

Lie on my grasses,
my rosebay, my lichen.
Lie on my mosses,
the softest of all.

What if I'm lonely,
fine forest, fair forest?
What if I dream
of returning to town?

You won't be lonely,
fair dreamchild, my wanderer.
With fox cub and grey dove
you won't be alone.

POMPEII

24th August, A.D. 79

The giants are sleeping now
under a hot land
where the grey snow
has yet to fall
and cover all
with its dying dew.

The city is silent now
under a haze of blue
till the pedlar's cart
on the stone-clad street
calls the early few
for pot or shoe
and the slave from sleep.

The hillside is sunwashed now
where the lush vine
and the olives line
the summer slopes
of the giants' home
in an August dream
that has almost gone.

The gods are sleeping now
unaware
by the temple walls
and market stalls
of the city square . . .

And an ashen cloud
shrouds the breathless crowd
as the grey snow falls.

SUNFLOWER

guards my south wall,
a private sun.
Floodlights the whole garden,
warms tardy flowerbeds into life
in leafy July.

She turns to face the sun – we're told;
I know it's wrong.
Really the sun chases my Inca goddess,
jealous of rival gold.

LATE

You're late, said miss.
The bell has gone,
dinner numbers done
and work begun.

What have you got to say for yourself?

Well, it's like this, miss.
Me mum was sick,
me dad fell down the stairs,
the wheel fell off me bike
and then we lost our Billy's snake
behind the kitchen chairs. Earache
struck down me grampy, me gran
took quite a funny turn.
Then on the way I met this man
whose dog attacked me shin –
look, miss, you can see the blood,
it doesn't look too good,
does it?

Yes, yes, sit down –
and next time say you're sorry
for disturbing all the class.
Now get on with your story,
fast!

Please miss, I've got nothing to write about.

SCHOOL DINNERS

The greater-spotted brown baked bean's
not quite the humble bird it seems;
it lurks beneath the soggy greens
                              waiting to get you.

The green unruly jumping pea
has no respect for you or me;
it's bound to land on miss's knee
                              and she'll get you.

The brown-backed flying liverslug
is little better than a thug;
you think you're safe – don't be too smug
                              he'll get you.

The quiet skulking greasychip
looks innocent – that's just his trick;
eat thirds or fourths and you'll be sick
                              he'll get you.

The many-fingered crumb-y fish
looks friendly, as you might well wish;
but leave him lying on your dish
                              he'll get you.

TEACHER SAID . . .

You can use
    mumbled and muttered,
    groaned, grumbled and uttered,
    professed, droned or stuttered
               . . . but *don't* use SAID!

You can use
    rant or recite,
    yell, yodel or snort,
    bellow, murmur or moan,
    you can grunt or just groan
               . . . but *don't* use SAID!

You can
    hum, howl and hail,
    scream, screech, shriek or bawl,
    squeak, snivel or squeal
    with a blood-curdling wail
               . . . but *don't* use SAID!

               . . . SAID my teacher.

LINES

I must never daydream in schooltime.
I just love a daydream in Mayshine.
I must ever greydream in timeschool.
Why must others paydream in schoolway?
Just over highschool dismay lay.
Thrust over skydreams in cryschool.
Cry dust over drydreams in screamtime.
Dreamschool thirst first in dismayday.
Why lie for greyday in crimedream?
My time for dreamday is soontime.
In soontime must I daydream ever.
Never must I say dream in strifetime.
Cry dust over daydreams of lifetimes.
I must never daydream in schooltime.
In time I must daydream never.

SPACE-SHUTTLE

Monday
my Aunt Esmeralda
gave me one of those
s p a c e – h o p p e r s .
You know,
those big orange things
that you sit on and   s
they're supposed to take you to the s   t r
Didn't take me any further than   a
the lamp-post
and that hurt.

Tuesday
I gave it to my baby brother.
Do you know, he really believes
it's going to work!
Some people will believe
anything.

Friday.
Just had a postcard
from my brother.
From the moon.
It says
'Had a good journey.   '
See you soon.   s !
Just hopping off to M^{a}r

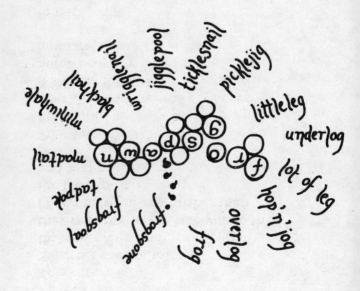

SNOW IN DECEMBER

Old willow fur-draped
against the winds; stars shiver
in a cool grey sky.

MAGIC MIRROR

Step before the magic mirror,
tell me what you see?

Could it be
 me, stretched tall,
 unfolded, gaudy blanket,
 giant transfer
 ironed to the wall,
 a sprawl of paint
 splashed in a dull hall
 by a lonely stair?

Could it be
 some painted circus clown
 blown from a nearby town,
 oil, marbled in a puddle,
 fuddled stained-glass window,
 Joseph's coloured coat,
 or splintered light
 from Noah's rainbow,
 low in a torn grey sky,
 after the storm?

Could it be
    Christmas crackers
    in wrappers tinselled
    and bright as a glass bauble,
    a summer garden
    dancing through rainy glass,
    waving flags, each one
    flown for a fair princess,
    or trembling wings
    of dragonflies,
    caught in August sun?

You look in the magic mirror,
tell me what you see;
is that really only – me?

JAPHETH'S NOTES: A FRAGMENT

Blue wash
drifting to grey.
First waterdrops
on father's up-turned head,
dew on a web of thinning hair.
Mist gathers over Ararat.

Voices of man and animal
up-pitched by fear.
Hammers drum a crescendo.
Plaintive duo of wolves howl
their elegy for drowning world.
Waters rise over Ararat.

Nostrils sharp with
gopherwood and pitch,
damp fur and panic-sweat.
Paws and claws jostle,
trail mud and excrement.
Sweet-sour smell
of ripening oranges,
fermenting grape
and olive oil.
Lord, may we safely
sink to earth on Ararat.

THEN

They never expected it of my grandmother,
all this choice.
Stolid, vocationally-trained
with neat samplers and clear instructions on
pastry-making and how to preserve the strawberries,
for forty years she happily baked my grandfather
rabbit pie, brawn, haslet;
collected fresh farm milk,
still-twitching pullets
and their warm muck-splattered eggs,
manure for the rhubarb, and mushrooms
dawn-gathered in chill Lincolnshire fields.

STABLE SONG

She lies, a stillness in the crumpled straw
Whilst he looks softly on the child, unsure,
And shadows waver by the stable door.

The oxen stir; a moth drifts through the bare
Outbuilding, silken Gabriel-winged, to where
She lies, a stillness in the crumpled straw.

A carpenter, his wife, both unaware
That kings and shepherds seek them from afar
And shadows waver by the stable door.

The child sleeps on. A drowse of asses snore;
He murmurs gently, raises eyes to her
Who lies, a stillness in the crumpled straw.

A cockerel crows, disturbed by sudden fear
As shepherds, dark upon the hill, appear
And shadows waver by the stable door.

The hush of birth is in the midnight air
And new life hides the distant smell of myrrh;
She lies, a stillness in the crumpled straw,
And shadows waver by the stable door.

REPORT

They said me grammar
wasn't too good.
She were all right
when I seed her last week.

He must learn to speak
proper, they said.
What cheek –
I can speak!
They should be glad
I'm there at all.

His sums ain't bad
though he has trouble
with his tables,
they said.

Me dad says
not to worry, lad.
Tables is for eatin' off,
he says.

Who's for a jam butty?

SEA SONG

Come sail the whispering seas, my love,
Come drift on the tides with me;
For I still long for the wild waves' song
And the silver fish of the sea.

Oh I'd sail the sighing seas, my love,
Where the wild weeds gently glide;
But I'm afraid of the forest shade
Where the silent fishes hide.

Don't fear the sauntering seas, my love,
As they dance beneath the breeze;
In the moonlit foam we'll make our home
Like the silver fish of the seas.

Oh I'll sail the rolling seas, my love,
And sigh for the cry of the wind;
But what if I weep on the ocean deep
To tread a greener land?

Oh you'll love the roaring seas, my love!
Come ride the swell with me,
Where the breaking sky is drawn to die
With the silver fish of the sea.

If I ride the raging seas, my love,
Then will you follow me?
Or will you stay till your dying day
With the silver fish of the sea?

Oh I must ride the wild, wild seas
And you must let me be;
Till my dying day I'll roam the spray
With the silver fish of the sea.

SPIDER'S SONG

See, I have stitched the ivy
with beaded threads of light,
a rich embroidery, newly hung.
Step on my tightrope,
lie with me;
let me fold you tenderly
in my pearled hammock,
lull you to silken sleep,
sweet dreamer,
under the dying sun.

MOSES – a sequence

SEARCHER

Princess, what are you dreaming,
down among the moist rushes?

Soft pleated linen, beaded bracelets,
purple grapes and Pharaoh's finest wines
await you at the palace –

yet you follow
a wavering baby's cry.

PLEASE, PHARAOH!

Pharaoh,
what use your
flutes and lutes now,
your bronze mirrors and
dancing girls in beaded anklets?

Locusts
have blackened
your figs, your corn
for bread, your dates and
grapes and pomegranates. Your crops

and rich
cattle dead,
river turned to
blood; for what good? Which
god will you call on now? And how?

A QUESTION OF PLAGUE

Pharaoh,
how do you like
frogs in your bed, locusts
gorging corn, boils too raw to touch?
Not much!

PLAGUE FROG

am
the frog
that leapt
from the Nile
that hopped
to the palace
that flipped
to the bedroom
that slipped
in the sheet
that flopped
with a smile
then nipped
at the feet
of the king who
kept Moses in Egypt.

COME ON, MOSES!

Sing to the Lord,
sang Miriam,
took her tambourine;
you've never seen
dances of such joy.
Soon after, hunger
erased the memory of
slave-drivers and whips,
Egyptian bosses, bricks
they ordered with no straw
offered, as many as before.
Hunger conjured onions,
crinkly cucumbers, melons
once enjoyed each day.
Someone had to pay,
and why not Moses?

Better die in Egypt, they cried
than lie in this desert, burn
in parching sun. Rather turn
again to Pharaoh. At least
we were fed. Maybe not free
but not dead either. Water, food!
Fetch us drink and find our bread!
Come on, Moses! Where's this god?

THE END

THE END